閱亮點
ENRICH SPOT

丁丁企鵝遊學館

有情有境學英語

學英語

04 活動篇 Activities

原作 江記 · 撰文 閱亮點編輯室

Contents
目錄

Meet the characters
角色介紹

Ding Ding
A little penguin. He is a lively kid who is ready to play at all times!

Mum
Ding Ding's mother. She always teaches Ding Ding to be a well-behaved child.

Dad
Ding Ding's father. He loves his family so much.

Mushroom

A friend of Ding Ding.
Her hairstyle makes her
look like a mushroom!

Glasses

Another friend.
He always wears
a pair of glasses.

Ryan

Ding Ding's cousin.
He is a mature penguin
for his age.

Masihung

A bear who wears a mask on his face.
He goes beyond lazy and
into super lazy!

Panda

A roommate of Masihung.
He is a conscientious panda. Sadly,
he is worlds apart from Masihung.

Watching television 看電視

1. What's on TV now?
   電視現在播放甚麼？

2. Literally 名副其實地

Watching the Olympic Games
看奧運比賽

1 Root for 打氣

2 Come on! 上啊！

3 Let's cheer for the athletes! 一起為運動員打氣吧！

Couch potato 懶洋洋的熊

1 Hurry up! 快一點！

2 Fell asleep 睡着了

Reading a book 看書

① Surprise
使人感到意外

② (Not) At all
一點也（不）

Playing jigsaw puzzle 拼拼圖

Busy

Hmm...

This jigsaw puzzle is too difficult to complete!

There are too many pieces. I want to give up!

Don't worry. You can always try again.

1 Difficult 困難

2 Give up 放棄

3 Try again 再試一次

Singing a song 唱歌

1 Sing along 跟著一起唱

2 Out of tune 走音

3 Tone-deaf 音痴

4 No way! 不可能！

Playing Chinese chess 下象棋

1 It's your move now. 現在到你下棋了。

2 Taking back is not allowed. 舉手不回。

Using an abacus 使用算盤

Mum, what is it? My new skateboard?

Let's count how many naughty boys there are.

No, it's an abacus. It helps you to do some simple calculations.

Haa...haa...

1 Skateboard 滑板

2 Do simple calculations 簡單運算

3 Count 計算

Using a computer
使用電腦

1 Watch livestream 觀看直播

2 Surf 上網

3 All day long 一整天

4 The Internet crashed! 沒有網絡了！

Cooking is really fun! 下廚真有趣！

The cookies are done baking. I've just got them out of the oven.

They smell good.

Now, let's share the cookies!

1 The cookies are done baking. 曲奇餅烤好了。

2 Smell good 好香

Playing a puppet 玩布偶

1 How cute! 真可愛啊！

2 Of course I do. 我當然（喜歡）。

3 Turn around 轉身

4 Isn't it better now? 現在好點了嗎？

Playing games 玩遊戲

There're lots of fun things to do at home...

...like playing the touch and feel game.

Hey, are you ready to have fun?

1 Are you ready to have fun? 你準備好一起玩了嗎？　**2** Bingo! 猜對了！

Drawing a picture 畫圖畫

① **That's cool!** 很好啊！

② **Gallery** 展示藝術作品的地方

Drawing outdoors 戶外寫生

Let's draw some flowers.

Great!

I indulged in the beauty of the scenery and did nothing... HAHA!

1 Indulge 沉醉

2 Scenery 風景

Art class 美術班

That's the end of art class. Let's clean the palette.

Rinse the paint thoroughly.

Ta-da! I've cleaned all the paint off.

But you've splashed the paint on me!

Haa! Haa!

1 Palette 調色諜

2 Rinse thoroughly 徹底沖洗

3 Ta-da! 嗒噠！（用作展現事物）

4 Splash 濺

Mindfulness meditation class
正念班

Panda, I've joined the mindfulness meditation class.
Come on! Pay attention to your breath.
You can feel it in your body as it comes in and out.
Hey, make sure you are relaxed and empty your mind.

Well, you're just being lazy.

1 Pay attention 關注（某事物）

2 Make sure 確保

Role play 角色扮演

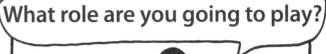

1 Do a play 演話劇

2 Play a role 演出一個角色

Watching a movie 看電影

1 Keep quiet 保持安靜

2 I bet 我相信 / 知道……

3 Right you are! 我同意！

4 Main character 主角

Playing basketball 打籃球

❶ Here you go! 給你！ ❷ It's show time! 是表現的機會了！

Playing badminton 打羽毛球

1 Go over the net （球）過網了

2 Stand still 站著不動

3 Time's up 時間到了

4 Burn my fat 燃燒脂肪

Playing table tennis 打乒乓球

1 Return this shot 接這一球   2 Retrieve 救（球）

Windsurfing 玩滑浪風帆

1 Hold on tight! 抓緊啊！

2 Choppy 波濤洶湧

3 Fell off 掉下來

Riding the bicycle 踏單車

1 Cycle track 單車徑

2 Get out of my way! 讓開啊！

30

Having a birthday party
開生日會

1 Elder 年長的

2 Come true 實現、成為現實

Sharing with friends
跟朋友分享

This photo is awesome!
I'd love to share it on my page.

I rather share it face-to-face.

1 Awesome 很好

2 Rather 寧願、更喜歡

3 Face-to-face 面對面

Chinese New Year 農曆新年

We're on Chinese New Year holiday now.

How do you like it so far?

It's great, especially when I receive red packets.

1 How do you like it so far? 到目前為止你覺得怎樣？

2 Red packet 紅封包（利市）

Let's eat the mooncake under the moon.

Nice. I'll have a quarter.

But Dad... where is the moon? It's the morning.

Look! There are moons in every pieces.

1 Mooncake 月餅

2 Quarter 四分之一

3 Every pieces 每一件

Mid-Autumn Festival 中秋節 ②

Dad, can we take a walk in the moonlight?

Sure. Go ahead.
Let's get the lanterns ready.

Hey, it's raining outside.

Come rain or shine, we'll play with lanterns tonight.

1 In the moonlight
在月光下

2 Go ahead.
就這樣做吧。

3 Come rain or shine
不管怎樣、風雨不改

35

Halloween 萬聖節

1 Do trick or treat 去玩「不給糖果就搗蛋」

2 Scary costume 可怕的服裝   **3** Dress up 裝扮

Christmas 聖誕節

1 It's freezing. 這裡冷極了。

2 Mittens 連指手套

3 Let's party! 一起盡情狂歡吧！

4 Decorate 裝飾

Graduation Day 畢業日

1 Gown 長袍

2 Anymore （不）再

3 Move up to primary school 升上小學

4 Sigh 歎氣

有情有境學英語 04 活動篇 Activities

原作	江記（江康泉）
撰文	閱亮點編輯室
內容總監	曾玉英
責任編輯	Zeny Lam & Hockey Yeung
顧問編輯	Sarah E.Williams
書籍設計	Stephen Chan

出版　　　閱亮點有限公司 Enrich Spot Limited
　　　　　九龍觀塘鴻圖道 78 號 17 樓 A 室
發行　　　天窗出版社有限公司 Enrich Publishing Ltd.
　　　　　九龍觀塘鴻圖道 78 號 17 樓 A 室
電話　　　(852) 2793 5678
傳真　　　(852) 2793 5030
網址　　　www.enrichculture.com
電郵　　　info@enrichculture.com
出版日期　2021 年 12 月初版

承印　　　嘉昱有限公司
　　　　　九龍新蒲崗大有街 26-28 號天虹大廈 7 字樓

定價　　　港幣 $88　新台幣 $440
國際書號　978-988-75704-4-8
圖書分類　(1) 兒童圖書　　(2) 英語學習

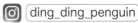

ding_ding_penguin